This book is donated to the Library in honor of Miss Tschanz on Boss's Day, October 2001.

All Things
Bright
and Beautiful

All Things Bright and Beautiful

Cecil Frances Alexander

illustrated by Bruce Whatley

HARPERCOLLINS*PUBLISHERS*

All Things Bright and Beautiful

Illustrations copyright © 2001 by Bruce Whatley

Printed in the U.S.A. All rights reserved.

www.harperchildrens.com

Library of Congress Cataloging-in-Publication Data

Alexander, Cecil Frances, 1818-1895.

All things bright and beautiful / Cecil Frances Alexander ; illustrated by Bruce Whatley.

p.   cm.

ISBN 0-06-026617-1 — ISBN 0-06-026618-X (lib. bdg.)

1. Nature—Religious aspects—Christianity—Juvenile literature.   2. Praise of God—Juvenile
literature.   [1. Nature—Songs and music.   2. Creation—Songs and music.   3. Hymns.]

I. Whatley, Bruce, ill.   II. Title.

BT695.5 .A42   2001   00-050560

264'.23—dc21   CIP

                                                                                          AC

Typography by Al Cetta

1 2 3 4 5 6 7 8 9 10

❖

First Edition

For Paul, Diane, Josh, and Sam

with a special thanks to Sally

—B.W.

All things bright and beautiful,
All creatures great and small,

All things wise and wonderful,
The Lord God made them all.

Each little flower that opens,
Each little bird that sings,

He made their glowing colors,
He made their tiny wings.

The purple-headed mountain,
The river running by,

The sunset and the morning
That brightens up the sky,

The cold wind in the winter,
The pleasant summer sun,

The ripe fruits in the garden,
He made them every one.

The tall trees by the greenwood,
The meadows where we play,

The rushes by the water,
We gather every day:

He gave us eyes to see them,
And lips that we might tell

How great is God Almighty,
Who has made all things well.

All Things Bright and Beautiful

Refrain. Cheerfully

All things bright and beau - ti - ful, All crea - tures great and small,

End

All things wise and won - der - ful, The Lord God made them all.

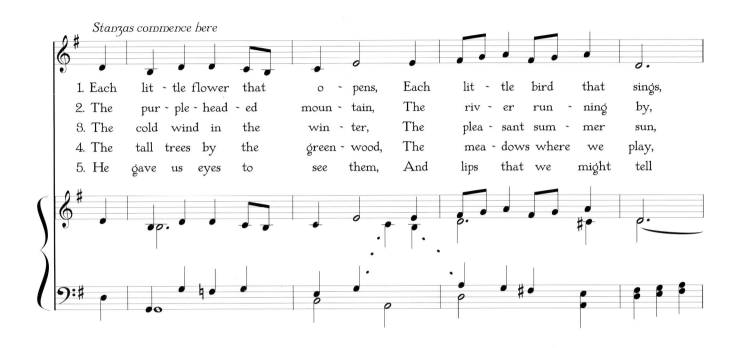

1. Each lit ~ tle flower that o ~ pens, Each lit ~ tle bird that sings,
2. The pur ~ ple ~ head ~ ed moun ~ tain, The riv ~ er run ~ ning by,
3. The cold wind in the win ~ ter, The plea ~ sant sum ~ mer sun,
4. The tall trees by the green ~ wood, The mea ~ dows where we play,
5. He gave us eyes to see them, And lips that we might tell

He made their glow ~ ing col ~ ors, He made their ti ~ ny wings.
The sun ~ set and the morn ~ ning That bright ~ ens up the sky,
The ripe fruits in the gar ~ den, He made them ev ~ ery one.
The rush ~ es by the wa ~ ter, We gath ~ er ev ~ ery day:
How great is God Al ~ migh ~ ty, Who has made all things well.